To the children at Weehawken Public Library,

Arrgh! Read on me hearties!

Tim Hopper

Pedro
the Pirate

Written by
Tim Hoppey

Illustrated by
Dianna Bonder

For Ellen, my green—eyed girl. ♥ Tim.

A special thanks to Trevor for his wealth
of boat knowledge and great reference material.
And, to my two amazing daughters who
watch so patiently as I work. ♥ Dianna

Text ©2012 Hoppey, Tim
Illustration ©2012 Bonder, Dianna

Hoppey, Tim.

Pedro the Pirate / written by Tim Hoppey; illustrated by Dianna Bonder.
—1 ed. — McHenry, IL ; Raven Tree Press, 2012.

p. ; cm.

SUMMARY: Cabin Boy Pedro yearns for the life of a pirate. When the chance
comes, he realizes that the life of a pirate is not for him.

English Edition
ISBN 978-1-936299-18-8 hardcover

Audience: pre-K to 3rd grade.
Title available in English with Spanish sprinkled throughout.

1. Action & Adventure/Pirates — Juvenile fiction. 2. Values & Virtues/Social Issues —
Juvenile fiction. I. Illust. Bonder, Dianna. II. Title.

Library of Congress Control Number: 201031376

Printed in Taiwan
10 9 8 7 6 5 4 3 2 1
First Edition

Raven Tree Press
A Division of Delta Systems Co., Inc.
www.raventreepress.com

Free activities for this book are available at www.raventreepress.com

Pedro wanted to be a pirate, but he was only the cabin boy.

Captain Crossbones was the real pirate and everyone feared him. Sailors on other ships trembled and screamed, "The pirate! ¡El pirata!"

Captain Crossbones had stolen his pirate ship. He had even stolen the parrot that sat on his shoulder.

The parrot repeated every word the captain said. When the captain bellowed, "My boots!" the parrot would squawk, "¡Mis botas!" Captain Crossbones didn't understand a word the parrot said, but Pedro did.

Pedro sat at the bow of the ship. He daydreamed about being a real pirate and finding treasure. In the distance he spied rocks that glittered with gold! "¡Oro!" Pedro yelled.

Captain Crossbones bellowed, "What the blazes did you just say?" "Gold! I said gold!" Pedro sputtered. "Arrgh, treasure!" the captain shouted. "¡Arrgh, tesoro!" the parrot squawked. "Quiet, parrot!" the captain shouted. "¡Silencio, loro!" the parrot squawked.

Captain Crossbones ordered the pirates to lower a boat, and he ordered Pedro to row it.

"Row!" the captain shouted.

"¡Rema!" the parrot squawked.

"Quiet, parrot!" the captain shouted.

"¡Silencio, loro!" the parrot squawked.

Pedro felt like a real pirate with real treasure
when he found a locket on the rocks.
"It's **my** locket now," he told himself.

Suddenly, a green-tailed girl appeared.

"How can you take what doesn't belong to you? Didn't anyone teach you that stealing is wrong?" she asked.

"It's what we pirates do!" Pedro boasted.

She looked at him, and a tear slid down her cheek.

Pedro thought the tear glistened like a jewel.

14

"I'd like to steal your tear, too," he laughed.
Then he cast a net and caught the girl.

15

"Arrgh, a fine pirate you'll be," Captain Crossbones said.
Pedro beamed and said, "If we keep the girl,
the mermaids will give us all of their gold."
"Good idea!" the captain shouted.
"¡Buena idea!" the parrot squawked.
"Quiet, parrot!" the captain shouted.
"¡Silencio, loro!" the parrot squawked.

17

Pedro tied up the
green-tailed girl and
climbed into bed.
However, that night
he couldn't sleep. Her
words haunted him.
"Stealing is wrong,"
she'd said.
He opened the locket.
Inside it read:
"To Elena, with love."
Pedro's heart was heavy.

In the morning, the mermaids brought bags of gold for Elena's release. Pedro smiled. "Now Elena will be free." But Captain Crossbones double-crossed the mermaids. He kept the gold **and** the girl. "It's all mine!" the captain shouted. "¡Es todo mío!" the parrot squawked. "Quiet, parrot!" the captain shouted. "¡Silencio, loro!" the parrot squawked.

21

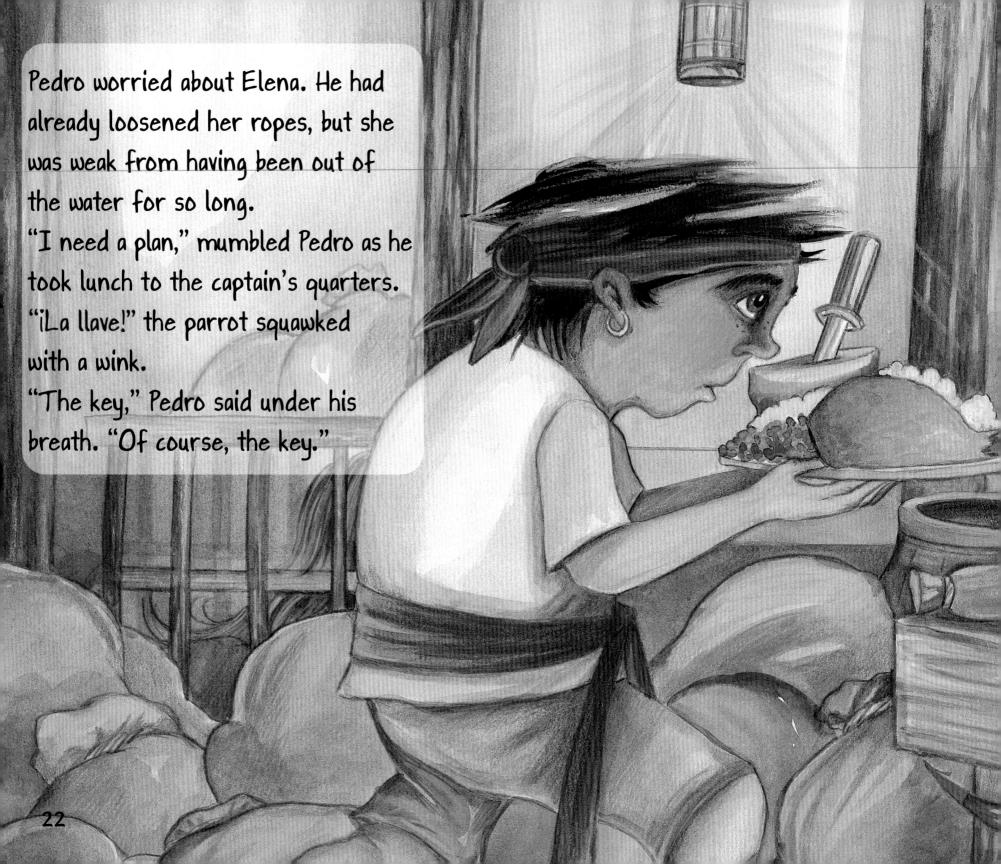

Pedro worried about Elena. He had already loosened her ropes, but she was weak from having been out of the water for so long.

"I need a plan," mumbled Pedro as he took lunch to the captain's quarters.

"¡La llave!" the parrot squawked with a wink.

"The key," Pedro said under his breath. "Of course, the key."

"Captain, why keep the mermaid? All she does is eat our rations. Let's have her walk the plank and be done with her," Pedro cleverly suggested.

The pirate agreed and took Elena to the bow of the ship.

24

In one quick motion the mermaid slipped out of the knots. She dove into the water and swam away.

Captain Crossbones squinted at the rope with his one good eye and growled, "Arrgh! At least I still have the gold!"

That night, Pedro crept into the captain's quarters.
"¡Silencio, loro!" Pedro whispered.
"Quiet, parrot!" the parrot repeated in English as it
lifted its wing to reveal the key.
Pedro took the key and with one click, the key opened
the treasure chest. He quietly carried the bags of gold
to a boat and lowered himself into the sea.

26

Pedro emptied the bags of gold back onto the rocks. Some of the coins plunked into the ocean and sank.

Pedro held out the locket.
"I was wrong, Elena.
I don't want to be a pirate."

30

There was a splash as
Elena appeared. She smiled,
and a tear slid down her cheek.
Pedro thought it glistened like
a jewel. But Pedro vowed never
to steal anything again...
except perhaps a heart.

31

Vocabulary	Vocabulario
pirate	el pirata
gold	oro
my boots	mis botas
treasure	tesoro
row	rema
quiet, parrot	silencio, loro
good idea	buena idea
it's all mine	es todo mío
key	la llave